발행일/2006년 7월 15일
펴낸곳/(주)한국삐아제 펴낸이/박종관 출판등록/1991년 7월 6일(제1-1226호)
주소/경기도 고양시 일산동구 식사동 288-29
고객 상담실/080-501-7991
www.piaget.co.kr

Pas peur du tigre
Copyright ⓒ 1999 Mijade Publications
Text ⓒ 1999 Laurence Bourguignon
Illustration ⓒ 1999 Laurence Henno
All rights reserved.
Bilingual edition, English/Korean rights ⓒ 2002 by Korea Piaget Co., Ltd.
This bilingual edition published by arrangement with Mijade Publications
through THE agency, Seoul, Korea

이 책의 영어/한국어판 저작권은 THE agency를 통한
Mijade Publications와의 독점 계약으로 한국삐아제에 있습니다.
저작권법에 의해 한국 내에서 보호를 받는 저작물이므로
무단전재와 무단복제를 금합니다.

ISBN 89-543-1762-6 ISBN 89-543-1951-3(세트)

Laurence Bourguignon / Laurence Henno

A Friend for Tiger

KOREA PIAGET

William skipped along the street, while he threw his toy tiger up in the air. "Jim, we're going to the circus. I want to see the wild animals and Sultan, the scary rabbit-eating tiger!"

"Three front-row seats, please!" At the circus, William bought the tickets.

It was crowded and noisy inside the circus. The circus ring was bright with lights.

The ringmaster walked into the ring.
"Hello, everyone!" he shouted, "welcome to the great circus show!"

불빛이 환히 비치고, 시끄러운 서커스 무대에 사회자가 올라왔어요.

윌리엄은 술탄이 나오길 기대했지만, 곡예사들이 먼저래요.

"Mommy, will I see Sultan, the tiger, now?" William asked.
"Not yet," said Mommy. "The acrobats come first."

곡예사들의 멋진 앞재주기에 관객들은 환호성을 질렀어요.

The acrobats showed off their flips and turns. They walked with their hands.
The crowd cheered as they left the ring.

그 다음에는 세상에서 그네를 제일 잘 타는 토끼 가족이 나왔어요.

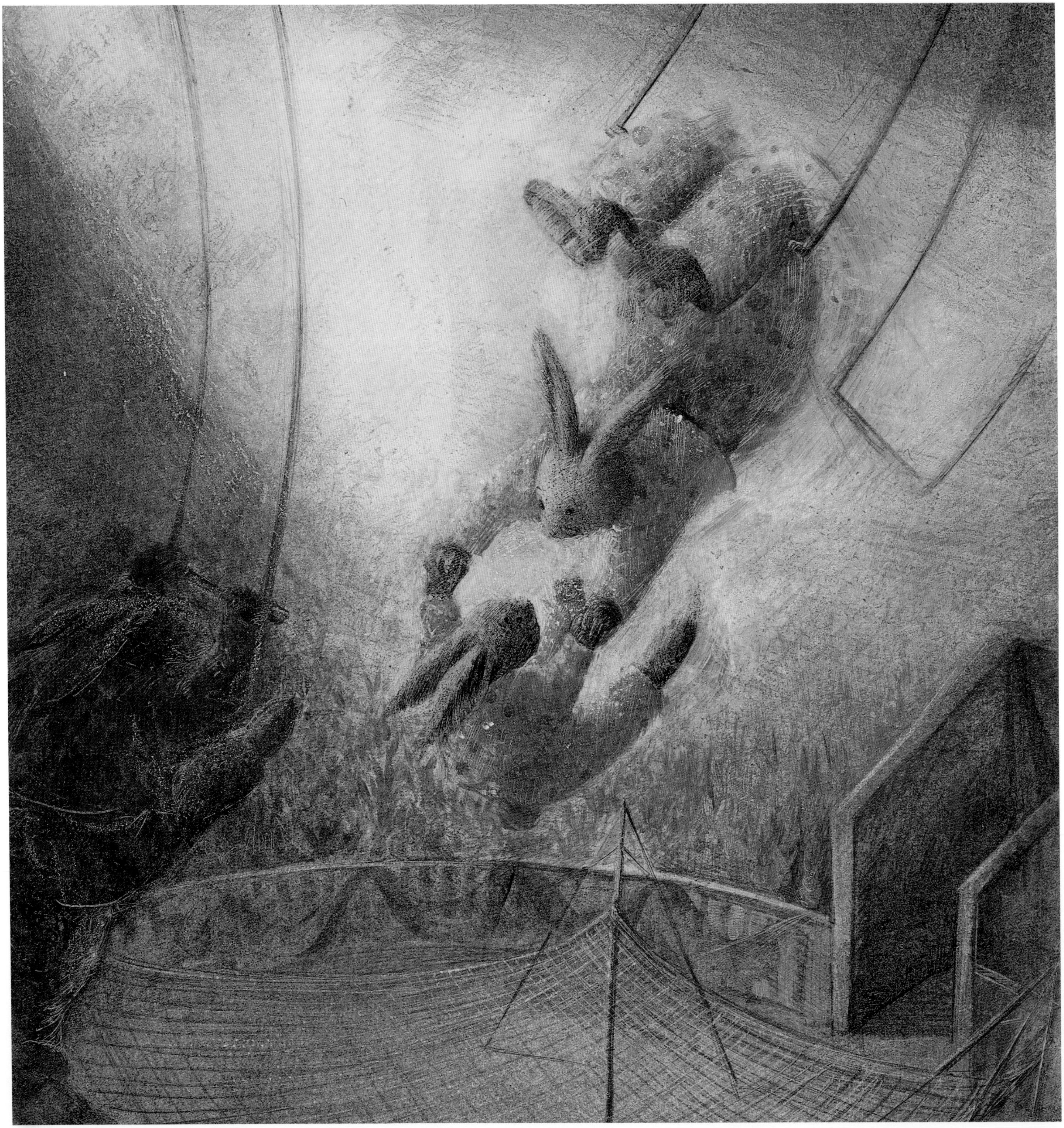

"Mommy, will I see Sultan now?" William asked.
"Look!" said mommy. "It's the famous rabbit family.
They are the best trapeze artists in the world!"

"If they are so good, why do they need a net?" said William to Jim.
The crowd shouted, "Bravo! Bravo!" as the Rabbit gave a bow.

"Now is Sultan coming out?" asked William.
"Oh, here come the funny clowns!" said mommy.

The clowns made the crowd happy.
But William looked somewhere else.
He saw a big cage being built.
"That must be for the scary rabbit-eating tiger,"
William said to Jim.

재미있는 광대들이 관중들을 즐겁게 해 주었지만, 올라와은 술통이 들어갈 큰 우리가 닫들어지는 곳만 보았지요.

북 소리가 울리고 으르렁대는 호랑이 한 마리가 나왔어요. 그런데 울리엄에게 카는 그 호랑이가 그리 무서워 보이지 않았지요.

It grew dark and the drums rolled. William held his breath.
The lights flashed back on, and inside the cage was a huge tiger.
That tiger doesn't look very scary to me, thought William. It roared.

"Ooh, isn't that tiger scary?" said mommy. Crack! Crack! Went the whip.
The tiger slowly walked across the ladder high up in the air.

The tiger jumped to the floor of the cage.

The drums rolled again.
The tiger walked up slowly to the burning hoop.

"No! Don't do it!" Shouted William. Crack!
Suddenly, the tiger leaped and William buried his face in Jim's fur.
The crowd roared.

눈을 떠 보니 관중들이 환호하고 있었어요. 윌리엄은 솜틀이 우리에 점을 던져 넣어 주었어요. 솜틀에게도 친구가 필요할 것 같아서요.

William opened his eyes and saw the crowd cheering the tamer on.
Nobody even looked at Sultan.
He blew Sultan a kiss and threw Jim into the tiger's cage.

"Why did you do that?" Mommy asked.
"Because Sultan needs a friend. Nobody cares about Sultan," William said.

That night William went to bed. He worried about Jim.
'I hope Sultan will take good care of him.'

William could not sleep. He was lonely without Jim.

William imagined Jim tucked in by the tiger's side.
How happy they seemed to be!

윌리엄은 짐이 호랑이 옆에 행복하게 누워 있는 모습을 상상했어요.

점과 술탄이 친구가 될 거예요.

'I'm glad to know Jim and Sultan are friends,' William whispered.
'I'm sure they will take good care of each other.'

A few minutes later,
William fell asleep dreaming of his friends all night.